Ethel Turner

The Little Duchess and Other Stories

Ethel Turner

The Little Duchess and Other Stories

ISBN/EAN: 9783744751315

Printed in Europe, USA, Canada, Australia, Japan

Cover: Foto ©Andreas Hilbeck / pixelio.de

More available books at **www.hansebooks.com**

THE LITTLE DUCHESS

AND·OTHER STORIES

By ETHEL TURNER

Author of "Seven Little Australians" &.

THE NAVTILVS SERIES.

WARD LOCK & BOWDEN·LIMITED

LONDON·NEW YORK & MELBOURNE

1896

CONTENTS.

NOTE.

My thanks are due to the Editors of the Sydney "Daily Telegraph," "The Bulletin," "The Town and Country Journal," "The Windsor Magazine," and other periodicals, for permission to reprint some of the stories in this volume.

The Little Duchess:

and other Stories.

———◆———

THE LITTLE DUCHESS.

"The tale is as old as the Eden tree,
And new as the new-cut tooth."

HE was the clerk of the cash tramway, and when the rolling balls gave him a moment's leisure, used to look down from his high perch at the big shop beneath his feet, and, in his slow, quiet style, study the ways of the numberless assistants whose life-books thus opened to him so many of their pages.

Lately there had come to the place a slight, grey-eyed girl, who wore her black dress with such grace, and held her small head with such dignity, that he whimsically had named her to himself " The Little

Duchess." He liked to look down and catch a glint of her hair's sunshine when his brain was dulled with calculating change, and his fingers ached with shutting cash-balls and dispatching them on their journeys. And he used to wonder greatly how any customer could hesitate to buy silks and satins when their lustre and sheen were displayed by her slim little fingers and the quality descanted on with so persuasive a smile. There were handsomer girls in the shop, girls with finer figures and better features ; but, to the boy in his mid-air cage, there was none with the nameless dainty charms that made the little Duchess so lovable.

For, of course, he did love her. In less than two months he had begun to watch for her cash-ball with a trembling eager-ness, to smooth out and stroke gently the bill her fingers had written, and to wrap it and its change up again with a careful tenderness that no one else's change and bill received. He had spoken to her half-a-dozen times in all; twice at the door on leaving—weather remarks, to which she had responded graciously; once or twice about bills that she had come to rectify at the desk, and once he had had the great good fortune to find and return a handkerchief she had dropped. Such a pretty, ridiculous atom of muslin it was, with a fanciful " Nellie " taking up one quarter, and some delicate scent lending such subtle fascination that it was a real wrench for the lad to take the handkerchief from his breast-pocket and proffer it to her.

So great a wrench, indeed, that he proffered his love, too, humbly, but fervently, and received a very wondering look from the grey eyes, a badly-concealed smile, a " Thank you " for the handkerchief, and a " No, thank you " for the love.

He had kissed her, though, and that was some consolation afterwards to his sore spirit, kissed her right upon the sweet, scarlet lips which had said " No " so decidedly, and then, bold no longer, had fled the shelter of the friendly packing-cases, and beaten a retreat to his desk aloft.

That was nearly a fortnight ago; not once since had she spoken to him, and to-day he was feeling desperate.

It had been a very busy morning, and he had found hardly a second to raise his eyes from his work. The one time he had looked down she had been busy with a customer—a girl prettily dressed and golden-headed like herself. That had been at about ten o'clock. Before twelve her cash-box, with the notch upon it that his penknife had made, rolled down its line, and he opened it as he had opened it twenty times that morning; but this time it bore his fate. With the bill was a little twisted note, on which "John Walters, private," was written, and the boy's very heart leaped at the sight. Down below, customers wearily waited for change, and anxiously watched for their own particular ball while the *deus ex machina* read again and again, with eager eyes: " Please will you meet me at lunch-time in the Strand? Do, if you can. I am in trouble. You said you loved me." Then, as he began mechanically to manipulate the waiting balls, he looked down to the accustomed place of the little Duchess. She was pale, he saw, and her lips trembled oddly now and again. There was a frightened look in her grey eyes, and once or twice he thought he noticed a sparkle as of tears.

At lunch-time he actually tore through the shop and away down to the appointed place. She was there—still pale, still nervous and fluttering.

" Let us go to the Gardens. It's quieter," he said, putting a great restraint upon himself; then, when at last they were within the gates, " God bless you for this, Nellie ! "

" What ? " said the girl, with uncertainty, but not looking at the plain, rugged face that was all aglow with love for her.

" For telling me about the worry—asking me to come. Oh, God bless you, Nellie ! Now tell me."

She sat down on a seat and began to cry, quietly and miserably, till the boy was almost beside himself. At last, between the sobs, he learned her trouble, which was grave indeed. She and her sister had very much wanted to go to a certain ball, and, more than that, to have new dresses for it, of soft white Liberty silk, such as she cut off daily for fortunate customers. But her purse was empty, so, in their emergency, the sisters had hit upon a plan, questionable, indeed, but not dishonestly meant. The sister came to the silk counter and purchased thirty yards of silk, paying 15s. for it instead of £3 15s.

"That was on account; I was only taking a little credit, like other customers," said the little Duchess, with a haughty movement of the head. "On Saturday I was going to make out a bill for an imaginary customer, and send the £3 up to the desk to you. Don't imagine I would really wrong the firm by a halfpenny."

"Oh, no," cried the boy eagerly; "it's all right."

"That's not all." The girl began to cry again, hopelessly, miserably. "I had no money to get the dresses made, and the next customer paid £2 10s., and—and—I only sent 10s. up to you—I wanted to make it just £5 I had borrowed. I thought I might borrow enough, as I was borrowing— don't forget, I would rather have died than have stolen the £5, Mr. Walters."

"Of course, of course, I understand," said the cash clerk, seeing it was a worse fix than he had imagined, but longing to take her in his arms and kiss away the tears.

"And then that horrid Mr. Greaves, who signed first in a hurry, asked for my book and took it for something, and then sent it up to the desk, and the figures are all confused, and the check-leaf isn't the same as I sent to you. I hadn't time to make it right, and when the books are compared to-night it will be noticed, and I shall get into trouble—and, oh, I am so miserable!" The little Duchess was sobbing pitifully.

He kissed her, this time in earnest; on

the lips, the cheeks, the hair, the tear-wet eyes. He only recollected himself when a gardener's form, and especially his smile, obtruded themselves upon their notice, and they sat apart looking foolish until the two o'clock bells made them hurry back to the shop.

"I'll put everything right — don't you worry," he said; and she smiled relievedly and went to her counter.

That afternoon he did what all the other years of his life he had deemed it impossible for him to do. He made a neat alteration in his books so that the £5 in question would not be missed. To-morrow, he resolved, he would take £5 of his own and pay it into the account of the firm. The little Duchess should be his debtor, and run no more risks. But, alas, for the morrow!

Before he had fairly taken his seat in the morning — before Nellie had finished fastening at her neck the violets he had brought her, — some words were said at his elbow, and he slowly became aware that he—surely it was a dream!—was being arrested for defalcations in his accounts. He learned that for some time past the firm had been aware of considerable discrepancies in the books, and had placed a detective-accountant in the office. Last night, for the first time, the man had discovered, as he thought, a clue, and had convinced the firm that in Walters he had found the offender.

The lad was ashen pale, horror stricken, as he realized how these things must go against him. He could not drag in the name of the little Duchess—even if he did, it would not avail him much; he certainly had altered his books, and to mention the girl's share would only be to have two of them brought to trial, and perhaps to gaol. The little Duchess in gaol! That hair catching the prison-yard sunshine! That slender form clad in the garments of shame! The boy drew a deep breath, gave one very wistful glance at the silk counter, and then walked straight to the manager's room, followed by the policeman.

"I took the £5 yesterday, and brought it back to-day. On my oath before God, sir, I have never misapplied one farthing of my moneys."

His voice trembled in its eagerness, the deep-set eyes gleamed, and the white lips worked.

"Your purpose, Walters?"

The manager looked hard, disbelieving.

"Direst need. Oh, believe me, sir, I have served you three years honestly as man can serve—yesterday I borrowed this money and brought it back this morning—don't ruin my whole life for that one act."

"Your pressing need yesterday?"

John drew a deep breath again.

"I—can't well tell you."

Then the heads of the firm came in, indignant at their misused trust, and they scorned his story. The defalcations amounted to almost £50 in all, and he had confessed to £5, which had been found

upon him. Of course, he and no other was
the offender, and they must teach their
employés a lesson. So John walked down
that long shop by the side of the official,
his head very erect, his face pale, and his
knees shaking: all his life he would remember the glances of pity, curiosity, and
disdain that met him on every side. As he
passed the silk counter, the little Duchess
was measuring a great piece of rose-red,
sheeny satin, that gleamed warm and
beautiful beneath her hands. She was very
white, and in her eyes was a look of abject
horror and entreaty; his eyes reassured her,
and he passed on and out of the door. All
his life he would remember that rose-red
satin and its brilliant, glancing lights.

After the trial everyone thought him fortunate to get only two years, and the little
Duchess, who had grown thin and old-
looking in the interval, breathed freely as
she read the account in the papers, and
saw that her name was not even mentioned
in connection with the matter. He wrote

B

to her a loving, boyish letter, and told her she must be true to him till he came out, and that then they would be married and go away where this could never be heard of.

It was no small thing he had done for her, he knew; and, as he was not more than human, he expected his reward. And the little Duchess had cried quietly over the letter, and for several days cut off silk and satin with a pensive, unhappy look that quite touched her customers—those few among them who realized that it was human flesh and blood at the other side of the yard measure.

*   *   *   *   *

Twenty months later the little Duchess was at the same counter measuring silk and satin for the stock-taking, when a note was brought to her in a writing she remembered too well.

"I got out to-day, Nellie Come down to the Gardens in the lunch-time."

She hesitated when the time came, but he

might come to the shop, and that would never do. So she put her hat on thoughtfully and set out for the Gardens.

He was awaiting her on the seat where, nearly two years ago, the gardener had smiled at them. He stood up as she came slowly towards him, and for a minute they gazed at each other without speaking.

She was in black, of course, but fresh and dainty-looking, with a bunch of white chiffon at her throat, little tan shoes on her feet, and her hair showing golden against the black of her lace hat.

For him, his face had altered and hardened; the once thick, curling hair was horribly short, his hands were rough and unsightly, his clothes hung awkwardly upon him, and his linen was doubtful.

"The little Duchess!" he said, dully; then he put out his hand, took her small gloved one, and looked at it curiously.

"I—I am glad you're out," she said, carefully looking away from him.

"Yes—we must be married now, Nellie;

that's all I've had to think about all this awful time."

His face flushed a little and his eyes lightened.

"It's good not to see the walls," he added, looking round at the spring's brave show, then away to the blue sparkle in the bay and the glancing sails.

"We mustn't talk of that time, though, ever—eh, Nellie?"

"No," she said, regarding her brown shoes intently.

His eye noted the smooth roundness of her cheek, the delicate pink that came and went, the turn of the white neck.

"Aren't you going to kiss me, Nellie?" he said, slowly; and he drew her a little strangely and awkwardly to him.

Then she spoke.

"I knew it wouldn't be any use, and you'd never have any money or get a place after this. We couldn't be married on nothing, and it would only drag you down to have me, too. I'm not worthy of you."

"Well, little Duchess," he said, softly, as she stopped and faltered; a slow smile crept over his face, and his deep-set eyes lighted up with tenderness.

Not worthy, his little Duchess!

Then the crimson rushed into her face, and she flung up her head defiantly.

"I married the new shop-walker, four months ago!"

WILKES OF WATERLOO.

WILKES OF WATERLOO.

MRS. JOHNSON had just bought an ornament duster from a Chinaman, and little Mrs. Wilkes had stepped over to admire it.

Mrs. Johnson had no ornaments to dust except an emu's egg and a child's gilt mug, but that was a detail. The duster was composed of soft magenta feathers on a burnished handle, and was a thing of beauty though its price was only eleven-pence.

" I'd fix it on the wall for a nornmunt," said little Mrs. Wilkes, fingering it affectionately. " Wha's it fer, proper ? "

" Dustin' the chiny and things in a drorin' room," said Mrs. Johnson, who had once been housemaid at Pott's Point.

Mrs. Wilkes laid it down with a sigh.

"I wish I'd got one," she said. "Only Wilkes would say 'luven-pence oughter buy a pie-dish or a broom."

Mrs. Johnson gave a disdainful sniff.

"Johnson knows his place too well," she said. "Why, he'd never dare remark on it even. Your man wants settin' down a bit, Mrs. Wilkes, as I'm often tellin' you."

Mrs. Wilkes sighed again. It was a long, deep sigh this time, and comprehended her "man," magenta feather dusters, and an infinitude of things; but, in the midst of it, the clock at the post office struck six.

"I've bin 'ere gone an hour," she gasped. "Wilkes gets 'ome at six fer tea."

Mrs. Johnson followed her to the door and laid a hand on her shoulder.

"Now, don't you be a little gowk," she said. "'Usbands 'as got to be taught they can't be brutes."

"Ev course," said Mrs. Wilkes; but she was trembling.

"An' if a woman can't step round and see a body, friendly-like, and have a little chat, what's the use of not bein' slaves an' 'Ottentots, say I?"

"Oh, ev course," assented Mrs. Wilkes; but she twisted herself gently away from her friend's grasp.

"Ev course, and I'll come round to-morrow, too ; but I'm just wondering like where little Tom is ; so I think I'll be goin'."

She walked slowly and with as much dignity as her little thin figure was capable of till she was well out of sight of Mrs. Johnson's following eyes. Then she broke into a run and sped like a hare up the two back streets to her home, and opened the door with a beating heart.

Wilkes was home. He was a tremendously big man, almost a giant in height and breadth of shoulders, and he seemed to fill the little room. He had a five-year-old boy on his knee, and there was an anxious, tender look on his square, determined face as he looked down on him and wiped away the tears that were flowing down his chubby, dirty cheeks.

"What's up, Tommie boy?" said Mrs. Wilkes, creeping in and taking off her bonnet in a shame-faced way.

Wilkes raised his head and gave her a slow, steady look out of his brown, keen eyes. "Where've you bin, Em'ly?" he said quietly. Emily remembered the precepts of Mrs. Johnson, and took courage.

"It's a pretty thing if a married woman can't slip round and see a friend in a way," she said in a small but determined voice. "I'm not a-goin' to stick in for ever and ever."

Still Wilkes looked at her in that quiet, strange way, and her eyes drooped and she began fidgeting about the table and straightening things for tea.

Tommie had stopped crying, and his father was brushing the dust off his clothes and looking at a bruise on his arm.

"What's the matter with 'im?" said Emily, aggrievedly; "an' look at his nice coat, all torn. I'll beat you Tom, you bad boy, you." Wilkes stood up and set little Tom on his feet.

" There was no one home, and he went to play near the station," he said. " He's bin knocked down by a cart."

"Tom!" shrieked Emily, darting upon her child and gathering him up into her little shaking arms,—" Tom,—little old Tom—oh, Tom, my little baby!"

She kissed him and sobbed, and sobbed and kissed him for two or three minutes.

" He's not hurt," said Wilkes.

She gave the lad a little shake. " You bad, dis'bedient boy; ain't I forbid you times and times to play out in the street?" She brushed some more dust off his sleeve and touched the bruise tenderly.

" I'm goin' to beat him fer it," said Wilkes, taking down a long, fairly thick strap from the top of the dresser. " You must always obey, Tom, my boy."

Emily knew from long experience it was worse than useless to protest, so she went to the other side of the dresser and stopped her ears while the beating went on. She was trembling too, but it wasn't for little Tom.

" There ! " said Wilkes ; and he pushed the screaming child gently into the bedroom adjoining, and shut the door. " Now, Em'ly."

"I won't," said Emily, clinging with desperate hands to the dresser. "I'm a growed woman; I won't be beat, Tom—Tom I tell you I won't."

She faced him, her cheeks white, her eyes blazing.

"Cum 'ere," said Wilkes quietly.

" I won't," shrieked Emily.

He pulled the small clinging hand away from the dresser, and drew her into the middle of the room.

" I'll tell the perleece—I'll get you 'ad up," she sobbed, struggling uselessly.

" You're my wife, Em'ly girl," he said quietly, " and when you won't do things fer askin', I've got to learn you."

He administered the beating, sharp enough in its way, and then put the strap high up on the dresser again.

For a time she sat on the floor with her head on a chair and sobbed convulsively, little Tom, the other side of the door, chiming dolefully in. Meanwhile Wilkes finished laying the cloth and got everything ready in a quiet, neat fashion : when the kettle boiled, he took down the little brown tea-pot.

"How much do you use?" he asked, pausing with the tin in his hand.

There was a sob from the other end of the room.

"Em'ly!" he repeated.

She raised her head a minute. "Two t—t—teaspoonsful," she said.

Little Tom recovered speedily, came out of retirement, and made a cheerful meal of German sausage, with bread and jam for a second course.

Emily was surprisingly hungry, but would not eat for a long time, though her husband pressed her, and even spread the jam on her bread himself.

"Don't be sulky, Em," he said, putting it in front of her, and sugaring her tea as she liked it; "you know I only do it for your own good, old woman."

But her poor little shoulders were still throbbing badly, and she pushed her plate back in a heart-broken way.

Presently, however, his tenderness prevailed, and she forgave him tearfully, and even ate three slices of bread and melon jam.

And by the time small Tommie was in bed, and they had washed up and tidied the kitchen between them, they were the best of friends again.

    *   *   *   *

But Mrs. Johnson's influence was not to be so easily undermined.

The next day Emily did not go round to see her as promised, so she just "stepped up" herself.

"Well, did Wilkes slate you much for not havin' his tea ready?" she asked, as she sat down in the spotlessly clean room.

"Oh, no!" said Emily, in surprise. "Oh, no,—he never said a word."

Tommy looked up from the boxes at which he was hammering. "He beated me," he said, "and then he b——"

"Go and play tram-guards in the yard, Tommie," Emily said, hastily; and Tommie, after much protesting, departed.

"Wilkes never touches you, I suppose?" asked the visitor, looking curiously into the little quiet face before her.

"Oh, lor', no," said Emily. "Gracious me, I should think not. He never laid a finger on me in his life."

But two days after that Tommie was asked to go and play with Mrs. Johnson's little boy, and there were buns and bananas and other nice things to eat. And Mrs. Johnson, with their kindly help, managed to find out from that transparent little party a true account of what had happened the night in question. She reproached her friend for her want of confidence in her, till Emily, in a weak moment, made a clean breast of it all.

"Wilkes is so awful big," she said, pitifully, at the end of the recital. "How can I help it?"

This was the kind of thing that was as the breath of life to Mrs. Johnson, and she

C

forthwith set to work to convert this new pupil from the exceeding error of her ways.

"Show more spirit, my dear. Don't you knuckle under," were her most constant injunctions, and Emily soon began to show signs of progression.

She bought a red feather duster and a big bow of pink chiffon instead of paying the baker's bill one week. But Wilkes only shook his head, and asked her pleasantly not to do it again.

Then she came home late for tea once more, and he was very angry, but only warned her.

"You must teach 'im a lesson, once and for all," said Mrs. Johnson. "Just assert yourself, my dear—assert yourself; that's what you must do."

"But he'll beat me," said the poor little wife; "an' you don't know 'ow it 'urts."

Mrs. Johnson deliberated a moment. "If he touches you again, you send for a bobbie. He could be 'ad up for wife beatin,' you know."

"Oh—h—h!" gasped little Mrs. Wilkes.

"Of course, you wouldn't like him to get

long ; but I'll warrant if he was run in for a couple of days, he'd never touch you agen while he lived."

"Ah—h—h !" said little Mrs. Wilkes.

Three days later there was a picnic at Botany—Sir Joseph Banks' Pavilion,—and Emily told her husband, in a defiant kind of way, that she wanted to go.

"You can't," he said shortly ; "I ain't a goin' to 'ave you gaddin' off with all sorts of folks without me."

"I shall go," muttered Emily rebelliously.

"Yes, you do," he said warningly, and went off, banging the door behind him.

Before she had time to think better of it, Mrs. Johnson came up for her. She dressed herself and little Tommie very quickly, and sallied forth with great courage. It was seven o'clock before she returned from the day's outing and neared home again. She had drunk several glasses of cheap claret at the picnic, and her silly little head was swimming.

Mrs. Johnson accompanied her as far as

the door. "Tommie," she said, "if yer pa attempts to beat yer ma to-night, jest you run out and call in a bobbie."

"All right," said Tommie. He had enjoyed the unlawful pleasure immensely, and had no objection to getting even with "pa" for sundry remembered beatings.

"I'll be hangin' round," she added, as Emily stopped at her own door and gave a half-frightened glance at the window. "There's a perleece just down the street. I'll see you safely through this; now's the time to strike for your rights. Just you show 'im you've got some spirit, Mrs. Wilkes. Don't you let 'im use you as he likes."

"Ev course not," said Mrs. Wilkes, opening the door and going in with Tommie.

It was nearly twenty minutes before the door opened, and the little boy slipped out.

"He's beatin' ma awful, with a big strap," he said to Mrs. Johnson, who had already given the constable to understand that he might be wanted in a particular house before very long.

The three of them went in together—
the outcry was sufficient to warrant it.

Wilkes did not take the slightest notice
of their entry, but went on using the strap
vigorously, and Emily shrieked as if she
was being killed. The constable, at her
entreaties, made an effort to prevent it, but
he was only a slightly-built man.

Wilkes turned round and looked at him
for a second. Then he picked him up
quietly by the collar of his coat, put him
outside the door, and assisted Mrs. Johnson
to the same place. "I'm not half through
yet," he said, as he closed it in their faces.

He had just finished, and replaced the
strap on the dresser-top, when they returned
with more help and arrested him.

"You'll have to appear against him to-
morrow," said one of the constables to
Emily, who was still shrieking with rage,
pain, and fright.

"Rather," she sobbed. "B — b — big
br—brute!"

*　　　*　　　*　　　*

The next day went by like a kind of nightmare, and evening found Emily alone with Tommie in the little house.

She had wept ceaselessly all the time in court, and had at first declared he had never beaten her. But then they reminded her what perjury was, and she admitted that he did sometimes, " but only for my own good."

The sympathies of the court naturally went with the little frightened-looking woman, with her blue, tear-drowned eyes, rather than with the stubbornly-silent Hercules in the dock, and they gave him seven days for wife-beating and resisting the constable. Emily had to be carried out of the court in hysterics, and assisted home by the ubiquitous Mrs. Johnson.

" It'll learn 'im a lesson, it will," the woman said as they reached the door.

But Emily turned suddenly round, lifted her little, work-marked hand, and struck her across the face.

" I h—h—hate you!" she said, and fled away into the safety of her own house.

The seventh day came at last, and the tiny house was awaiting its master. The tins, polished to unnatural brilliancy, stood in shining rows; the dresser was scrubbed to snowy whiteness; there was a bright fire in the well-blacked grate, and a tempting little feast was spread on the flower-decked table. At one end there were no flowers, and a little space had been cleared for the strap, which lay, like a brown, coiled snake, ready for action. Only Tommie was in charge, for Emily had gone up to Darlinghurst to wait for her husband.

He stepped out from the great gaol, and a little figure sprang to his side.

"You!" he said.

"Yes, please, Tom; I've been waiting for you four hours."

"Um," he said, and walked on in silence for a long way, trying not to show the glad relief in his face.

"Aint you comin' 'ome?" She looked at him anxiously. "Dinner's waitin', Tom dear, and I've got tram tickets all ready."

Still he walked on in silence.

"I don't know as there's any use comin' 'ome ever again, Em'ly," he said at last.

She clasped her hands round his old coat sleeve. "Tom," she whispered passionately, and pulled his head down to her,—"Tom, you can beat me till you kill me, if you like."

They caught the Waterloo train and went the rest of the way in silence. Then Emily opened the door and drew him into the shining, fire-lit room.

Small Tommie was asleep by the fire and Wilkes glanced at him tenderly.

"When I like, Em'ly?" he said.

"Yes, yes," she answered eagerly.

"Now?"

She came and stood before him with bent head, and he beat her softly about the shoulders. She looked up at him with smiling, tear-wet eyes.

"Now put it in the fire, Em'ly," he said. And she took it from him and laid it gently right in the heart of the glowing coals.

AT A STREET CORNER.

AT A STREET CORNER.

THE footsteps of the crowd were in his ears, the voices of it, its sighing and its laughter. His fingers lay motionless across the raised letters of the great book on his knees, and his eyes were strained forward, but they saw nothing but his own misery.

It was the only thing in the heavens above and the earth beneath that he had ever seen.

They thought he was asleep, the tram-waiting crowd around, for his head had fallen a little forward on to the placard he wore upon his breast, and his lips were quiet.

And the crowd went home, little by little, till the corner was nearly deserted, but he did not move. Then there came a slow, shuffling step along the foot-path,—the step of the old, old man who sold papers daily at the same corner. And the money-box, near the great book, was suddenly grasped by a thin old hand, and the shuffling steps went away rapidly and died in the distance. But the boy sat motionless. Almost a smile parted his lips.

"No one ever stole from me before," he whispered to himself, and lifted his head a little as if the act had placed him for once on an equality with a world that always pitied. He smiled faintly again. There must be someone in the city as miserable as himself if one had come to such a pass as to steal from him.

But the next day this mood had passed, and nothing but bitterness was in his heart.

And when the slow, shuffling step came past again, and he thought of the comfort the stolen money would have brought, a very demon came into him.

He stood upright in his place, and laid

the money-box and the great book down
on the ground; he took two quick steps
in the direction of the slow, shuffling ones,
felt for the figure that carried the news-
papers, and knocked it heavily down across
the pavement.

The nerves of the crowd were immeasur-
ably shocked. The great book lay in the
dust; the old man was slowly raising
himself in injured surprise, and there was
the blind, young, passionate face before
them, or they would have thought their
eyes had played them false.

There was a man of the church amongst
them, and he went forward and laid a quiet
hand on the boy's sleeve.

But the young face was still ablaze, and
the poor, wild eyes straining forward.

"Let me go," he said, trying to free
himself.

But the hand still held his sleeve and
the colour dropped from his face again.

"I am blind," he said, as if the calamity
had just come upon him.

They led him back to his seat and placed him upon it gently, and laid the book on his knees again.

"Read," the man of the church said softly, and the boy opened the great book and laid his quivering fingers on the first page.

"And God said, let there be light," he read.

Then his voice vibrated.

"And God said, let there be light," he repeated.

But no one even expected him to finish the sentence.

TO
THE CITY OF RASPBERRY JAM.

TO
THE CITY OF RASPBERRY JAM.

"Sydney to Hobart in 53 hours. Large boats. Every possible comfort."—*Vide Shipping Advertisements.*

IT was on the wharf—the Sydney wharf—they smelt it first.

"M—m—f," said the Person of Importance.

"Hidden Ambrosia," said the Girl with Imagination, gazing raptly at a tarred barrel.

But "Scrimmy!" was the remark the Long-legged Boy made. He had poked an inquisitive penknife through the canvas, and it had come out red with—raspberry jam.

After that they explored the wharf in excitement; huge cask after cask stood there filled with raspberry jam to the brim. You would have thought all Sydney was going to

D

spread its bread on both sides with the delicacy, three meals a day for the next half-year. You would have been afraid Hobart had left itself nothing but empty lanes in its endeavours to satisfy the hungriness of its northern sister.

It was after noon, almost time for the vessel to start—advertised time. But steamship companies allow three hours of grace for parting tears occasionally, so ample opportunity was afforded to count the barrels a thousand times and weary of the perfume. And when the third hour came and no start was made, the Long-legged Boy begged leave to translate "jam satis" in the way of his historical schoolfellow.

The "Oonah" heard him, and moved away with as much dignity as fussiness and foam would allow.

The wharf fell back, back. Soon it was black and irregular, with little white waving lights that meant "God-speed" and tears— possibly "happy riddance."

Two little girls with flying hair waved

energetic farewells to the big house on Kirribilli Point. They were the admiral's daughters, also going Raspberry-land-wards.

The Bishops had a jaunty look. They were bent on business, of course—the great Church Congress was to be held in the little island-city — but there was a nice little holiday stretch between, so they might be allowed to smile.

The Heads grew less and less important looking. Here were the ocean bays, happy hunting ground of the Sydney picnicker, seen from a new point of view. How the waves leapt against Coogee cliffs! What a sweep of beautiful beach Bondi showed! And that little field, white-dotted, that sloped down to the blue waters—what was that? Field glasses were levelled. Hush! only the little Waverley city of the dead with its thousand gleaming head-stones.

Laughter on deck, jesting voices, eyes a-brim with purpose and hope, merriment or thoughtfulness—life.

And across there the little white field, asleep for ever.

Botany Bay. Listen, one of the long black coats is speaking.

"When Captain Cook first landed here, Sir Joseph Banks, an eminent botanist in the party, was—— "

But the Long-legged Boy moves away hurriedly.

"Page 2, Australian History, Simpson, Mondays and Fridays," he says. "I say, d'ye suppose they ever have dinner on this old tub? Holy Moses! Isn't that woman a little premature?"

Truly it seemed so. She was a steerage passenger, over on the second deck, and she was crouching against a heap of canvas in an attitude of complete dejection. Her head had fallen sideways, her bonnet was hanging by its strings, she kept a feeble hold of a rope hard by.

The number of women on any deck has grown small by degrees and beautifully less.

There is a bell at last. "Only dressing,"

groans the Boy with Long Legs; but soon it rings again. No one makes an elaborate toilet.

A saloon full of men ; here and there a brave female—only here and there. Few smiles, fewer jests ; it is a serious business this first meal. There are a thousand and one strange mingling smells, a moving floor, and a dull thud — thud of waves against the wall. It is a time when it is legitimate to take heed to what we shall eat and what we shall drink. See the grave faces bent over menu cards, which might be last wills and testaments of wealthy relatives from the way they are studied. There is a run on boiled fowl, also boiled fish—both sound, plain and wholesome, and harmless.

"Pickled pork, madam ?—y—yes," says the steward behind the Person of Importance. Privately, he does not think much of her complexion; but to hear is to obey. She tries feebly to tell him it was an extra fork she asked for; but he is gone.

Then she says wanly, to no one in particular, that she "thinks she will go on deck now, for a little time."

So she goes, with not an atom more dignity than a Person of No Importance. The Long-legged Boy helps her upstairs— not cheerfully, but of necessity. Then he comes back and studies the menu again. The Girl with Imagination is also on deck. She has a far-away look in her eyes. She says she did go down to dinner, but it struck her she was missing the beautiful coast scenery, so she came up again. She talks a little about the blue haze on the hills, and the little leaping waves, and the sunset lights, and then grows pensive again —pale, someone said; but, then, that was the natural effect of imagination.

A Young Man with a Moustache comes up; he says he doesn't believe in heavy dinners, and he also mentions his reluctance to miss the coast-line.

It seems incumbent to discuss heaven and earth, and the musical glasses, but they do so gloomily, and with an unhappy feeling of insecurity.

The Young Man with the Moustache asks if she has read "Trilby."

The Girl with Imagination thinks of the discussion likely to ensue, and says "No," mendaciously.

The Young Man speaks of the cleverness of "Some Emotions and a Moral"—"What does she think of Cynthia as a specimen of womanhood?"

The Girl with Imagination "Has'nt read it"—in a tired voice.

The lights on shore glancing here and there are Bulli, then Wollongong; a wind springs up, and the waves freshen and give joyful little pokes to the boat. There is a long silence, and when the Young Man hears it, he asks if she has read Shakespeare.

The Girl with Imagination says "No," at first, desperately; then she remembers Washington's cherry-tree, and adds, "he is a beautiful writer"; then she moves away and stretches herself quite horizontally on a lounge.

Such a swell it is! The vessel rises and falls, slowly, feelingly; groups break up, everyone goes to gaze upon the phosphorus, or to lie down flat.

Overhead the clouds drift up, and put out the twinkling lights, one by one; the wind waxes stronger, and the waves climb higher and higher up the sides.

A female figure comes up the companion —the stewardess, long-suffering and of great kindness.

"You must come below, ladies," she says. "It is very late. You will be better in bed."

The Person of Importance says she is going to stay up all night.

The Girl with Imagination finds herself thinking longingly of a bed in a churchyard that never moves an inch; all other beds seem loathly. But the stewardess prevails, and has the satisfaction of tucking up in their berths two of the most miserable women in the world—two women who have asked themselves, more in sorrow than in anger, why they were ever born, and been unable conscientiously, to reply.

Morning again ; such a white sea ! Only a few go to look whether the coast-line has run away : the remainder lie prone in their berths and pray for the end.

Later on a bell rings. It is the dinner bell trying to speak churchfully : in point of fact, as two Bishops are on board, to say nothing of other black coats, there is going to be a church service in the social hall. Sorrow and gloomy meditation have convinced a few that they have souls ; so they scrape up the courage necessary to walk across the lurching deck and down the steep companion. There is a scarcity of hymn-books and prayer-books, and to stand steady looks easier than it is. The piano sails along. Two or three who have no books know the words ; the others open their mouths and sing tee-ti-tee-to-tee-too-te-tum in reverent tune, and with pious expression. Then the Sydney Bishop gives a short homily, in the midst of which one or two take hurried departures; perhaps his words went home.

After that everyone sings " For those in peril on the Sea," and there is a thrill of self-pity in some voices.

Deck again, the coast-line has vanished altogether; there is nothing but a " waste of angry billows tossing," as the poetry books put it.

A hundred and nineteen passengers, and not two among them happy with the happiness that belongs to perfect security!

The Person of Importance says plaintively she came all the way from England and was not sea-sick for five minutes—" horrid little boat."

Someone with gold buttons says squally weather like this is unheard-of at this time of year, and he is not surprised that even the best sailors succumb; the short coast trips are far more trying than long voyages.

The Girl with Imagination respects herself once more, and the Boy with Long Legs eats a passion fruit.

The little girl with flying hair brings four of the same dainties from her pocket; she offers the Bishop a much crinkled one.

He is sitting on a very high camp stool, with a rug shawlwise over his reverend shoulders, and a macintosh tucked round his gaitered legs. He sucks the fruit with much solemnity, and asks for another. Then he is suddenly "called away," and the smallest girl with flying hair tries not to smile.

It is Rochefoucauld who says there is something in the misfortunes of our best friends that does not displease us.

The bell again, quicker and more importunate in sound this time.

> To eat or not to eat, that is the question,
> Whether 'tis wiser for the sick to suffer
> The pangs and troubles of a hungry feeling,
> Or to take food in recklessness and laughter,
> And, after eating, sorrow. To eat, to grieve;
> To grieve—ay, there's the rub.

The saloon tables are not well filled. The steward comes up for deck dinner orders He offers the menu card, but the Person of

Importance reads it through with a smile that is sadder than any tears, and orders "biscuits and a tomato." The Girl with Imagination requests a "pillow and a rug."

> You have heard the beat of the off-shore wind
> And the thresh of the deep-sea rain.

All the afternoon they swept over the deck, sheets of blown rain, gusts of shrill wind. Everyone has gone down but half a dozen men and the Girl with Imagination. The latter is getting drenched, but she has weighed the cabin and untold misery against a wetting, and decided in favour of clean, wholesome rain.

How it sweeps down! It looks for the meeting-place between collars and headdress, and pours chillily in between, and down unhappy backs. The men pull up their collars; one of them insists that the Girl with Imagination shall go to the lower deck —"no place for petticoats," he says.

But the lower deck!

> This is Hades, manifest, beholden,
> Surely, surely here, if aught be sure.

Everyone is bad here—it is only a matter of degree. From the Bishop to the youngest baby, high and low, great and small, thin and fat—they have all abandoned any attempt at keeping up appearances and are abjectly unhappy.

Darkness again, slow of approach; no stars to-night—nothing but tossing waters and a grey, cloud-swept sky. The morning and evening are the second day.

Soda water is the great breakfast delicacy the third] day, with or without dry biscuit. It is taken for the most part in the privacy of the cabins.

" Hunger, I beg to state,"

says the Long-legged Boy after an un-satisfactory visit to the saloon,

" Is highly indelicate ;
That is a fact profoundly true,
So learn your appetite to subdue."

"What you see," says Carlyle, "yet cannot see over, is as good as infinite."

The Girl with Imagination is certain

there are twenty-four hours to each of the sixty minutes of this third day.

Four o'clock in the afternoon is getting-up time to the early risers to-day; more fashionable ones put in their first appearance at six. But oh! such a coast! New South Wales and Victoria had been soft lines of hills rising and falling, tenderly blue while the sky was fair, and mistily grey through the rains and storms. This is magnificent.

Straight walls of wild rock dropping sheer into the waves, pillars of dark massiveness, waterworn into a thousand fantastic shapes; deep sepia shadows, indicating caves; frowning mountains, with their heads near the sky that softens now the day is dying.

A violet flush creeps up and spreads. Just where the mountain tops tower, it deepens into purple, and the banks of clouds burn gold at the edge. Over the rugged slopes the delicate mists hang, burnished, exquisite, like the filmy, wonderfully embroidered bridal veil over a harsh, plain face.

Twilight on the waters—English twilight, loth to give place to night. All the red and blue gone from the purple, tender, shadowy grey on hills and sky and sea. A sea grown gentle again—musical, coaxing; almost like a child, penitent and sweet and tearful after a stormy burst of anger.

Then " lights in the darkness, sailor "—will-o'-the-wisp lights among the shore trees, a fisherman's boat shooting along the shore, a lantern that shines and disappears.

More lights, steady-burning and bright.

The Person of Importance adjourns to her cabin to set her bonnet at the angle orthodoxy insists upon; the Girl with Imagination puts on one glove and sighs; the Long-legged Boy enumerates the things he intends to have for supper.

Flying stewards, wide-awake sailors, passengers unseen all the voyage, an atmosphere filled with portmanteaus and cabin boxes, tin trunks and repositories for best hats.

Nearly in. Black wharves looming out

on to the paler waters—one particular wharf alive with people and lights.

In she glides, thankfully, alongside. Three times the rope misses; then the Hobart ones catch it, and troubles are over.

" M—m—f," says the Person of Import-ance. " M — m — f, it's the very same smell; how remarkably strange ! "

The Girl with Imagination peers into the darkness. She has heard of a land flowing with milk and honey. Possibly this one leaks raspberry jam ?

But the Long - legged Boy bids her "Stop mooning. To-morrow," he says— " to-morrow we'll investigate this smell; but to-night, for the love of life, let us go and have a tuck-in."

TOYCHILD.

F.

TOYCHILD.

TOYCHILD sat on the top of the staircase, gnawing thoughtfully at a turnip. It was a remarkably dirty one, but she did not mind that; her eyes were fixed so intently on the rich red carpet at her feet.

What was the train of thought in that baby mind it would be hard to guess, but she got up suddenly with a funny little brow-pucker, trotted quickly down the corridor, till, near the servants' quarters, she came to a piece of bare-boarded floor, and then sat down all in a little heap.

Fanny, Mrs. Mountjoy's smart maid, found her here presently, when only a grimy stump of turnip remained.

"Get up," she said, enforcing the order with a poke of her foot.

"Go to the dev—vil," said Toychild, unmoved.

Fanny cuffed her smartly on the head and small bare arms, and Toychild kicked and struggled, but uttered no cry.

"S'pose I'll have to dress you before the missus comes," the girl said, subduing her at last, and driving her into a large, beautiful nursery. She pulled off the soiled frock, gave her a hasty soaping and polishing, and slipped on an elaborate silk frock.

"Now go down, you low little brat, and don't dare get dirty," she said as she finished, "and say, 'Thank you, Fanny'; you ill-mannered, common child."

"Damn you, Fanny," said the Toychild. Then she laughed—a shrill, baby laugh—and fled downstairs as fast as her wee legs would carry her.

It is rather a curious name, Toychild, is it not? Mr. Mountjoy, however, had bestowed it himself upon her, and surely, seeing he had bought her, he had a right to choose her name.

She had other ones, of course. Mrs. Mountjoy called her Gladys Claribel, and the child herself sometimes persisted piteously and tearfully that her name was Nan.

Mr. Mountjoy's name was really the most applicable; however, for a toychild she was, and, it seemed, ever would be, and this is how the thing had happened.

In one of the seasons when the world considers it the correct thing to be out of town, Mrs. Mountjoy, killing time at a mountain hotel, met in her walk a tiny bare-legged child, so wonderfully pretty and engaging, that she was enchanted. She hunted up the mother, and found her—a poor young thing of twenty-seven, with tear-sodden eyes and the mark of a blow across her cheek.

The child she admired was only one of six.

Mr. Mountjoy, at his wife's entreaty, entered into negotiations for the child with the husband, a rough, drunken fellow. He would adopt the child, bring her up in luxury and give them fifty pounds down (he often gave double that for a horse) to start them again in life.

The man agreed eagerly, and even the mother, after a few hopeless, miserable tears, nodded her assent. What chance had she to make the child happy? "I cannot allow any communication—the new life must have no connection with the old," Mrs. Mountjoy had said.

Again the mother cried a little; then she put her poor, white lips to the child's mountain bloom, kissed her fiercely, hungrily, despairingly, and pushed her across to her new parents.

And that is how little Nan became "Gladys Claribel," and the "Toychild."

Of course, Mrs. Mountjoy grew tired of her. She had wearied of her toy-terrier in a fortnight, her pony phaeton in a month, her riding horse in two. Nan lasted three months, and then spent long days in the beautiful nursery that had been fitted up, or in wandering about the big house, chased from place to place by the maid Fanny, who highly resented the extra work involved by a " beggar's brat."

Mr. Mountjoy had not tired so soon, but, then, he had not lavished undivided attention and worship upon her for two or three months, so his fire might be expected to burn a little longer.

He liked to have her follow him about the house like a pet spaniel, and ask funny little questions, and swear back at him in the way he had taught her. As soon as she grew obstreperous, he would say,—

" Here, Fanny, put your mistress's toy away, the paint's coming off."

And Mrs. Mountjoy would flush vexedly at the sarcasm, and, perhaps for conscience salve, have her in her room while she dressed for a dinner or a ball.

Just now she was riding a Theosophy hobby to a rapid death, and found Nan an unmitigated bore. She wanted to get rid of her, any way, any how, and suggested that the child should be packed off back to her mountain home.

But Mr. Mountjoy would not hear of it. It went against his principles to part with a fifty - pound investment after barely three months' use. There was the nursery, be-sides, and the toys and the clothes—it would be a clear loss.

Nan had been first delighted, then be-wildered, in her new home; then she drooped, lost her high spirits and bewitching little ways, and the days of neglect began.

The big rooms and splendid furniture seemed to oppress her poor little soul; the wonderful frocks and shoes made her un-comfortable, the handsome dolls and mechanical toys frightened her. She began to creep into the kitchen or yard—they had something familiar about them—and she evinced a passionate attachment to a washer-woman who came weekly, till Mrs. Mount-joy discovered it, and immediately sought to break it off, complaining vexedly of the child's low leanings.

That turnip had been a wonderful source of consolation to her to-day. She had found it in the dust-bin, and hidden it down the front of her muslin frock from the lynx eyes of Fanny.

It had a familiar, beautiful look. "Mover," who stood over steaming wash-tubs all day, used often to give a huge turnip to baby to stop it crying, and Mikey and Tim and she used to creep round and steal it.

> "Mikey an' Tim an' Molly an' Nan,
> Eat yer pertaters out a tin can,"

said Toychild in a little sing-song voice, as she rocked herself to and fro on the top chair, and sharpened her small white teeth on the turnip. She sang it again—

> "Mikey an' Tim an' Molly an' Nan,
> Eat yer p-p-pertaters out a tin c-can."

Then the round, grey eyes took a wild "remembering" expression, her underlip drooped piteously, and she ran down the passage to the patch of bare, familiar boards.

"Mover!" she cried, with a little frightened gasp.

Soon the recollection faded, and she cuddled herself together and gnawed away cheerfully at her turnip.

Now Fanny had disturbed and dressed her, and she was wandering forlornly about the hall. The drawing-room was forbidden ground—Mrs. Mountjoy had slapped her bare little arms for breaking a china ornament there; in the dining-room a Japanese butler was setting the table, and she was afraid of him; the servants all chased her out of the kitchen, and there was no garden.

A big Persian cat, prime favourite at present, crept out of the drawing-room, stretched himself and yawned—once he had scratched her.

A vicious feeling took possession of Toychild's breast. She would punish him. He began to wash himself amiably, blinking lazily at her the while. She swooped down on him and gathered him up in a determined fashion. He scratched her little, soft arms horribly, he spat and hissed, but she gripped him with Spartan courage, struggled to the goldfish bowl that stood in the outer hall, and flopped him in.

"There!" she said, and her grey eyes danced.

But "There!" snapped the cat; and he brought the bowl crashing to the floor, ate a couple of gold-fish, and retired kitchenwards to dry.

"Hum," said Toychild, thoughtfully. Then she dragged an umbrella from the stand—it was raining—and slipped out at the open hall door.

It was much nicer in the street. She unfurled the umbrella—it was Mr. Mountjoy's, a regular tent—managed to snap it in some way, and went sailing down the road. Such a wee, comical figure, with brown, tumbled curls, all wet with raindrops, and round eyes ashine with adventure; with naked little arms clasped tightly round the stick of the wind-filled umbrella, and be-socked little legs, struggling to keep a firm hold on the slippery pavement. No wonder people looked and smiled.

Two ladies stopped suddenly. "Why, it's little Gladys,—the child Mrs. Mountjoy has adopted!"

Toychild tried to push on.

"You must come home, Gladys,—you'll be lost! Come, we will take you to the door." One lady put a detaining arm round the small waist.

"Damn you; go to the dev-vil; tonfound you; bress my soul!" said the Toychild, struggling desperately. One lady looked horrified; the other held the child firmly.

"It's that Mountjoy,—he teaches her, poor little mite! Here is his wife's carriage—we will stop it."

In a couple of minutes the umbrella was down, and Toychild bundled into the carriage with her new parents, who were driving home from the races. Mrs. Mountjoy scolded her fretfully, Mr. Mountjoy looked at her gloomily, and then swore at his wife. He had lost heavily on a favourite horse, and the sight of the expensive toy irritated him.

In the hall all was confusion,—the floor was strewn with broken glass and ferns, gold and silver fish lay palpitating on the tiles; several of the servants were standing about, and the Persian cat, with a vindictive expression on his face, went and rubbed his wet body against Mrs. Mountjoy's skirts. Toychild tried to efface herself behind a chair.

"It's all that young imp," began Fanny.

Mr. Mountjoy pushed the small offender aside till she staggered giddily.

"Take her away, and punish her," he said; "and leave in a week yourself for not minding her."

Shrieking and swearing her very best, the child was borne off through the kitchens and out into the stable-yard, where her noise could not disturb the mistress.

Miss Fanny wreaked upon her a woman's angry spite, beating her poor little body, and leaving her alone to sob out her small heart in the darkness.

The next day, and the next and next, life went on as usual for Toychild, only there were strange shadows round the grey, childish eyes, and the soft under-lip got a habit of trembling and twitching oddly.

She abandoned the smart, smiling wax images in the nursery, and bestowed all the affection of her hungry little heart on a dirty rag-doll she had made from dusters, and kept carefully out of Fanny's sight.

And every day she would watch her opportunity, and steal into the laundry, and, with the rag bundle hugged closely to her, would creep into one of the tubs and cuddle up close to its cold side.

> "Mikey an' Tim, an' Molly an' Nan,
> Eat yer pertaters out a tin can."

Every day she would sing the doll this lullaby, and every day the soft eyes would grow round and frightened, and the yearning little cry go up to the laundry roof— "Mover, oh! Mover."

The air-spirits could endure it no longer. They bore the broken, baby voice away— up, up, where tall gums and wattle grew round a tumble-down cottage.

One day, a young shabby-looking woman, with a tear-sodden face, and the mark of a fresh blow across it, stole with uncertain step through the yard to the back door of the Mountjoy's town residence.

There was no one about; not even a servant of whom she might ask tidings of the child for whom her heart was aching.

She lifted her hand to knock at the half-open laundry door. Hush! what was that soft little sing-song voice inside?

> " Mikey an' Tim, an' Molly an' Nan.
> Eat yer pertaters out a tin can."

" Dod bress my soul — tonfound you; damn you, Mounty, go to the dev-vil. Oh, mover ! "

Mr. Mountjoy was standing within the stable after giving an order about a sick horse, when he saw an ill-dressed woman creep stealthily down the yard, looking with wild, affrighted eyes from side to side, as if fearful of pursuit, and hugging a great bundle covered with a shawl.

"Some of the plate, I'll be bound," he muttered, taking a stride forward. The next minute he laughed silently and fell back.

Below the shawl hung a wee, sturdy leg, with its white lace sock and small red shoe. He looked up and recognised the woman's face. She gained the gate, opened it trem-blingly, fearfully, closed it behind her silently, and fled away into the dark, falling shadows. He made no movement to follow her.

"Stealing her own child!" he muttered —the hungry, desperate look on her face haunted him—"poor beggar!"

Then he ordered a hot mash for the horse, and went inside to tell his wife.

A MODERN ACHILLES.

F

A MODERN ACHILLES.

JOAN was writing letters on pale pink notepaper. She had finished three, and there were nine more to be done. The corners of her mouth were drooping, there was an unhappy look in her eyes, and a dab of ink on the end of her nose.

"If it wasn't for my new muslin, I would try to bear it stoically," she said, and smudged a line with her sleeve; "but the thought of the wasted labour in those frills will embitter my whole existence—bother!"

The concluding expletive was called forth by the sight of the smudge.

"If only the jellies weren't made," Ella said. "That's what I mind most. That pineapple one was really beyond everything."

In the armchair there was a wet hand-kerchief and a crumpled girl in a short frock.

" It's wicked," she said ; " it's cruel. The only pleasure of my holidays. I've dreamed about it every night. And school next week. No boats, or twos and threes, or rounders, or anything."

Every word was a tear.

" Bother ! "

Joan had smudged another sheet. She pushed the desk away pettishly. " I'm not going to write any more of the horrid things ! "

" If only you weren't such prudes," the girl in the armchair said. " Do you imagine you're in a box, and all Australia's levelling its opera-glasses at you—who'd care ? "

Joan gave her an exasperated look.

" You're only a silly schoolgirl, Thea— think of the people we've asked ! Why, the Delany girls would faint at the idea of a picnic without a chaperone. There's no help for it. Do you think I'm not as disappointed as you are?" Thea made her handkerchief a little wetter, and her eyes a deeper red. Joan's reluctant pen scratched away again. Ella's jelly - regretful sighs floated about the room.

The picnic they had planned and dreamed of, cooked for, lived for, must at the last moment be declared "off."

The lady who was to have chaperoned the party had been inconsiderate enough to sprain her ankle just when all arrangements were completed.

Even the jellies were made, the pantry was full of cakes and delectables, and Joan had almost worn out the machine in her haste to finish an ethereal confection of muslin and lace.

Try as they would they could not fill up the place. The picnic was for Boxing Day, and among all their acquaintances in the district there was not one married lady obligingly disengaged enough to come and play propriety for them at such short notice.

Their father and mother had gone for a

Christmas trip to Tasmania, and had given permission for the picnic, providing only that it was suitably chaperoned. They had invited the guests—a couple of officers from a man-o'-war in the harbour, an Englishman " doing " Australia, with a drawl and a beautiful moustache, a young squatter, a bank clerk, and several girls, the daughters of very conventional neighbours. Clearly they could not go without a lady of a certain age, more especially as it would be a public holiday, and the Parramatta River, whither they were bound, would be alive with holiday-makers.

" I'd like to know what good they do," Thea said, in a voice so withering that even her tears checked themselves. " Why, last holidays, at the Gresham's picnic, there were three chaperones ; but it didn't prevent our Jack from squeezing Nellie Alton's hand, for I saw him."

" Our Jack " entered just in time to catch the last sentence, and to project a sofa cushion at the speaker. Had he not laughed and spoken, they would all have risen, and acted politely to him as to a stranger. Instead, they screamed at him, danced about, laughed uncontrollably, ceased for a minute, and laughed again.

" Sheep dog, at your service," he said, and minced across the room. He was dressed in a long, handsome skirt of his mother's, with a fashionable jacket, left unbuttoned, and a boa of black lace around his neck.

There was a grey, amazingly natural-looking wig on his head, and surrounding it a black jet bonnet, with an aigrette and long strings. A veil and pair of eye-glasses, a few deftly-painted wrinkles, and a languid smile completed his " get up."

" I'm going to see you through, girls," he said, as soon as he could put in a word edgeways between their laughter and exclamations.

Thea fell upon his neck, regardless of the diffident security of the bonnet.

" You darling," she sobbed ; " oh, you dear boy! you trump! you brick, Jack!"

Then she walked over to the writing-table,

took possession of the pink, regretful post-
ponements, and calmly dropped them into the
water of a great bowl of roses, seeing there
was no fire at hand, the thermometer being
at 9S degrees.

And that was how it happened that the
party was chaperoned by a clean-shaved
boy of twenty-two. They introduced him
as Aunt Emmelina, and he bowed beautifully or shook their hands gently, and
murmured correct little society nothings.

It came natural to him to do it well, for he
was an inimitable mimic and one of the best
amateur actors in Sydney.

But, at first, Aunt Emmelina considered
she had been unfairly used.

The girls had said Esther Hardress, the
present goddess of their brother's somewhat
mutable affections, could not possibly come,
as she had caught the measles from her
little brother, and was in bed. That was
the reason he had been willing to give up
his own pleasure, and do his best for his
sisters, for he did not consider any of the

Sydney Cowell

"'My dear friend Esther. Aunt Emmeline.'"

[Page 82.

other girls who were invited worth his attention. But when the morning came and the people began to assemble at the big house on the hill, in walked Esther, in a cool white dress and a sailor hat.

Aunt Emmelina, talking to the Delany girls at the end of the verandah, took a sudden stride from them and knocked down a hamper. The bank clerk and the squatter rushed politely to pick it up, and she said, " Thanks, old fellow," to the latter, and then tried to cough away the end of her sentence.

" You little sneak, Joan! " he said, in a fierce whisper, as his sister nudged his arm, and said " Be careful " with her eyes. " I'll get even with you for this." ·

Joan introduced them. " My dear friend Esther, Aunt Emmelina."

" I heard you had the measles, my dear," Aunt Emmelina said in a thin, old voice. She retained the hand, in its white suède glove, with all the tender solicitude of a chaperone of forty years' standing.

"Oh, no ; it was Edith who caught them
—my sister, not I," Esther said.

She managed to get her hand away, and
moved across the verandah, to be instantly
surrounded by the officers and the bank
clerk.

Aunt Emmelina went through the French
window into the breakfast - room, a sulky
look on her nice old face. Joan was there
putting some bottles of claret into a hamper.

" I've a great mind to chuck it all up,"
he said angrily.   " Making a fool of me
like this!   Why didn't you tell me she
was coming ? "

Joan caught his arm, hung on to it, imploring him not to give up now.   " We shall
be the laughing-stock of the whole neigh-
bourhood, Jack," she said, and there were
real tears in her eyes."

Somebody called her, and she hurried out.

Aunt Emmelina stood in moody silence,
her back to the fireless grate.   Thea came
in, all arms and legs and beaming smiles.

" Where's your corkscrew ? " she said.

"Why, what's the matter, Jack?" The last word was whispered.

"Oh, confound it all!" Aunt Emmelina said, and pushed up her veil regardless of consequences.

Thea went up to him and put her lips to his ear.

"It's Esther, is'nt it?" she said.

"Mind your business," he answered, and turned sharply on his heel, forgetful of his dress tail.

But Thea followed him up.

"Sometimes chaperones kiss the girls good-bye," she whispered, and fled out again among the others.

Aunt Emmelina put her veil down carefully, arranged her curls with diligence, and set her bonnet straight. There was a smile in her eyes behind the glasses. After all, there might be some enjoyment in the position.

Esther had evinced careless disregard for his ardent admiration lately, though once she had received it almost graciously.

As " Jack," he would have been pushed aside to make room for the squatter, of whom he had suspicions, for the officers— even for the bank clerk.

As " Aunt Emmelina," he might have the felicity of touching that white, beautiful hand of hers often ; he might even put his arm round her waist in a motherly kind of way.

And Thea was quite right. He had seen chaperones take quite an affectionate leave of their young charges at the end of a day.

So they set out. And surely in all the annals of chaperonedom there had never been quite such a charming, gentle, entertaining old lady as Aunt Emmelina.

They gave her the most comfortable seat at the end of the boat, and the squatter arranged her sunshade with great care.

" Come and sit here, my dear," she said, as Esther was guided carefully into the boat by the bank clerk. " Come and tell me about poor little brother."

Esther took the place rather unwillingly.

She had promised to sit on the same seat as the squatter, while the bank clerk rowed. Still, a chaperone has her privileges, and she was obliged to sit where requested, and talk measles with her.

There were three other boats, and Jack had seen that the good rowing men were equally distributed in them. In his own, however, the bank clerk was a very poor oarsman, and the squatter a great deal out of practice, so they were left somewhat behind.

They had started from Longnose, and were to go almost to the head of the river.

But the squatter had an unbalanced mind whenever Esther was anywhere near, and the bank clerk was in desperation at the untoward behaviour of the oars.

So it was hardly to be wondered at that they got into a mess before they reached their destination.

Just past Hunter's Hill a great sailing boat came bearing down upon them, and a steamer was close behind, but no one had noticed such details until it was almost too late.

Then the bank clerk grew pale and splashed frantically with his oars, and the girl with the steering lines lost her head, and forgot which side she should pull. The younger Delany girl, with beautiful wisdom, stood up in her place and screamed. Esther gave a little gasp and clung to the friendly arm beside her. But Aunt Emmelina thrust her roughly aside, and almost fell across the boat to the middle seat. She swept the bank clerk out of his place into a feeble, astonished heap, seized the oars, and with a couple of powerful strokes swung the boat round out of danger. Afterwards the bank clerk had a confused remembrance of being called "a confounded young idiot," and he resented it with an air of dignified surprise toward the chaperone for the rest of the day. He had old-fashioned notions of his own about women, and considered "dash it" and "bother" the extremest limit to which their language of exasperation might go.

Aunt Emmelina resigned the oars to the squatter when they were in clear water again, and seemed much troubled because she had burst her black kid gloves. She smiled at the surprise of the party at her act, and said simply she had been used to the management of boats since her earliest youth.

The morning passed as does the time at most picnics; they all did many things in general and nothing in particular, and waited for lunch to dissipate the slight air of restraint that not infrequently hangs over picnickers till chicken and salad, claret cup, and conversation peppermints, intrusive ants, and the paucity of plates do their genial work.

But when the meal was over, Aunt Emmelina felt very much what is popularly known as "out of it."

Esther was lingering over a bit of custard roll, and out of aggravation directing her conversation towards Miss Delany, and the squatter was lingering over Esther, and wishing Miss Delany at a further place. Joan was talking picnic nonsense with the two officers. One boat containing two people had already drifted away, and the bank clerk was persuading two girls to entrust themselves to the boat and his tender mercies again.

Aunt Emmelina was dying for a smoke.

If she could have talked to Esther she would have sacrificed the desire, but, as it was, she merely anathematised the squatter, and kept fingering the pipe and tobacco pouch she had carefully put in her pocket, till she could resist no longer.

" Would you like to come out in a boat with me, my child ?" she said, at last, gently to Thea, who was feeling somewhat exhausted after a prolonged attack upon cream cakes.

The little girl got up and followed her brother rather in surprise, and they pushed off together. Everyone remarked how well the old lady pulled, and Ella waved a relieved farewell from the shore. She was on

tenterhooks all the time, on account of the
vagaries of her " aunt." They soon passed
the first boat ; and when some distance away,
Aunt Emmelina rowed at a rate that would
fairly have electrified the picnickers could
they have seen.

Then she gave the oars to Thea, subsided
into the bottom of the boat, lighted her pipe,
and had a luxurious smoke that soothed her
injured feelings and ruffled nerves into
placidity again.

" It isn't many brothers would do what
I've done for you girls," she said, as Thea
pulled back again some hours later. " There's
Esther letting that fat-headed Barton dangle
after her all the time. I might have had
a chance if it wasn't for these wretched
petticoats."

He got out, and tied up the boat at a post
on the little shingly beach without waiting
for assistance.

" But fat-head Barton can't wish her good-
bye like you can," Thea whispered again in-
sinuatingly.

G

Two or three of the girls, Esther among them, had strolled some distance away and were standing on a boulder, idly throwing stones in the dancing water and watching the circles. The men were lounging around, smoking cigars, among the hampers, and talking to the other girls who had declared it was too hot to stir.

Thea rummaged about and found some bananas. She offered the squatter one, and kept three for herself, and they were all laughing and proposing a more equitable division, when a frightened scream broke the hot, quiet air over the river. Everyone sprang up and looked in the direction of the sound. Two of the girls were running frantically about, and the third was struggling in the water.

They all knew by the sailor hat bobbing about that it was Esther.

The squatter gave an answering shout, and started running at a great rate, taking off his coat as he went. But Aunt Emmelina shot along in front of him;

her skirts were gathered up in a rough bunch under one arm, her bonnet hung down her back by the strings, her glasses tumbled off, her hair wobbled about and fell in a grey mass over her shoulders. For one second, when she reached the rock, she tried to get rid of her cumbersome skirt, but the hooks resisted her, and she sprang straight into the river with a flop that might have been heard a quarter of a mile away.

But the squatter had caught up, too, and precipitated himself into the water; and now it was a question of who could reach Esther first, for she had floated some distance out. Jack knew himself to be no mean swimmer, but the skirts tangled his feet, and the tight jacket held his arms. The squatter was only a few yards behind: Jack struck out wildly and made rapid pace. But somebody seized him under the arms as he struggled for a moment to free himself from the jacket.

It was one of the officers, a better swimmer than either of them.

" My—dear—madam," he panted, holding
him in a firm grip and trying to swim back
with him, " Put your hand on my arm—so."

But Jack struggled madly away, and
made two more strokes, only to be caught
by the officer and fairly dragged back.

" Mr. Barton will save the young lady.
Do you want to drown yourself, madam ? "
The officer spoke in a tone of exasperated
patience, for he thought the chaperone was
a mild lunatic.

" Drown your grandmother ! " spluttered
Jack, swallowing a pint of water, as he freed
himself. " Can't you see who I am ? "

The squatter was ahead of him; he trod
water for a second, and flung off the jacket
that bound his arms.

He saw Esther was keeping herself afloat
without much difficulty, and he resolved he
would take her to the shore himself, or die
in the attempt.

He gained on the squatter; he received
the splash from his circling boots full in the
face, and the temptation for water-leapfrog

was too strong to be resisted. He trod water again, came up behind his enemy, planted his feet on his shoulders, and sent him downward with the greatest goodwill and energy. Half-a-dozen more strokes and he was alongside Esther.

"Jack—oh! dear Jack—oh! Jack!" she said, hysterically, as his wet, beaming face bobbed up beside her head, which she was trying to keep flat on the water in floating position.

"It's all right, little girl," he said, re-assuringly. "Everything's all right now. You're as safe as a church."

But she lost her presence of mind for a minute in her relief. He bade her put her arm on his shoulder, and she put them both without reserve round his neck.

"It's an ill wind that blows no——" he murmured, but the rest of the sentence was mingled with water.

He managed, however, to get to shore without much trouble, for she floated obediently, and he towed her.

The squatter had just clambered up a slippery rock, and was looking sulky, and the officer was shaking himself dry.

There was a general roar of laughter as Jack climbed out and lifted Esther from the water, little the worse for her adventure. He had left his bonnet, wig, and jacket in the water, and appeared in a white flannel shirt and long, dripping skirts.

Joan unfastened the hooks, and he kicked them off and stood before them attired in his boating flannels.

"Thank heaven!" he said, with pious fervour. He peeled off the remains of his split gloves and joined in the laughter. Then an adjournment was made for drying purposes to a cottage close by, and Esther submitted without protest to the supporting arm of her rescuer. The rest of the day was confusion and merriment, but there were five white minutes at the end that spread out afterwards over the whole lives of two people.

"How can I ever thank you?" Esther

said, and blushed beautifully, for she knew quite well the way she could.

"In a book," Jack whispered, "the hero and heroine would be sure to marry after such an adventure, and live happily to the end of their lives."

"Oh!" said Esther.

"And the heroine would be absolutely certain to reward the hero with a kiss."

"Ah!" said Esther.

The boyish face, full of anxious love, was close to her own.

"After all, it's only Aunt Emmelina," she said with a little trembling laugh as her lips touched it. Then she fled away down the garden path after the others.

He went into the house again, giddy with his sudden happiness.

"What did I tell you?" said Thea, dropping the corner of the window blind with a triumphant smile.

ON A PENNY FERRY.

ON A PENNY FERRY.

"And now if e'er by chance I put
      My fingers into glue,
Or madly squeeze a right-hand foot
      Into a left-hand shoe,
      I weep, for it reminds me so."

SOMEONE was giving an afternoon tea party on "The Shore," and it promised to be an unusually solemn and important affair.

No one masculine had been asked who was not figuratively or visibly long-haired; and no one feminine who had not a faint ink-stain on her right-hand fore-finger and a belief in Spiritualism in her soul. Naturally, nothing but conversation was to be indulged in, and strawberry ices and the latest thing in sandwiches were to be the reward.

I was all impatience to get to such a reason feast and soul flow, and quite chafed because the sea was " wet as wet could be," and the medium of a ferry-boat would have to be used.

But the seven or eight minutes' transit did not, after all, drag unduly.

I had hurried exceedingly to catch the boat, broken " into a run " across the quay, and hastened breathlessly through the turnstile and down the jetty, only to find there were still six minutes to the time of departure.

So I went past the cabin and outside up the bow to cool my warm cheeks and indulge in a little justifiable wrath against that curiously untrustworthy article — the feminine watch.

There was a very little girl at the end, and an oddly large boy; that is to say, for his age. He was in frocks yet, and had probably not seen more than three mosquito seasons. But he was surprisingly bulky and solid looking, and the babyish,

On a Penny Ferry. 103

wool cap surmounting his big, wide face, looked absolutely laughable. The girl, on the contrary, was the smallest creature imaginable. She had a little, old face, and tiny, bird-like hands that grasped tightly at an ancient, blue plush bag; and she kept one of her bright, eager eyes on the boy at her side and one on the dancing harbour and the ships.

"It's Frederick Thomas's birthday," she said suddenly, seeing that I was looking in a speculative fashion at the boy.

"Ah!" I said, startled by the abruptness of the announcement, for I had hardly recovered sufficiently to take the initiative in the conversation.

"An' we're goin' a voy'ge — ain't we, Frederick?"

Frederick Thomas only looked vacantly at his thumb which, for one brief moment, he had extracted from his mouth.

"Mrs. Jinks lent us the bag, and daddy guv us tuppence," she said, and a great, beautiful smile spread over her small, quiet face. "Ain't the 'arbor fine, and the ships? ain't this a fine ship? *ain't* we enjoyin' ourselves, Frederick?"

Frederick was still regarding his succulent thumb, and gave no answering speech or smile.

"Can't he talk yet?" I said, regarding the fat-headed child in a fascinated way.

"N-no," she said, very regretfully. "He's gone in the 'ed a bit, you see, and all gone in the legs—— " She paused and looked at him very tenderly. "But you can laff, can't you, Frederick?"

She bobbed her head up and down within an inch of his nose, she pinched his fat, bare legs, and gave an odd little whistle—"Diddums den, chuck-a-ruck-cluck, tom-timithy ti-chooral."

Over the wide, smooth face of the child dawned a faint flicker of a smile, his dull eyes disappeared in two folds of flesh, his toothless gums displayed themselves, his chin touched his chest. I turned away almost with horror, and hastened to add myself to the crowd already gathered at the side to be ready to land with a minimum of delay and a maximum of discomfort.

Up to the wharf the boat sidled, churned the water, flung out a rope, tossed down the gangway, and emptied itself. The last view I had of my little travelling companions was one hastily taken over my shoulder. They were up at the bow still, and seemed trying to efface themselves.

It was much more than an hour before I had a surfeit of soul, strawberries, and sandwiches, and was ready to return. By an athletic-looking engine-boy I had noticed, I knew it was the same boat in which I had crossed over. And at the boat-head Frederick Thomas and the Small Person were sitting in just the same attitudes as an hour back.

The Small Person's face grew crimson as I took my seat.

" *Don't* let on," she said, in an imploring voice. She caught at my arm with her little, thin hand.

"Oh! don't let on, there's a good 'un,— it's Frederick Thomas's birthday, or I wouldn't 'ave."

I looked at Frederick for a solution, but he merely showed me both his thumbs, which looked water-worn, like the fingers of a washerwoman.

" We rid each time—the man don't know, we ain't done no 'arm, 'ave we, Tom-tid-dums?" went on the little beseeching voice, "an' we guv one browny, didn't we, Tomothy? 'Ere's one fer goin' back."

She opened her hand and disclosed a bright penny. " Don't let on, I say."

I had an attack of coughing that lasted a minute or two. "You have been travelling backwards and forwards several times for that one penny!" I said as severely as I could.

The Small Person grew white, and put a protecting arm round Frederick Thomas.

" Are you goin' to get us copped?" she said in a voice that shook. Two big tears sprang into her wide, frightened eyes, and fell on Frederick's woollen hat; the chest under the old cotton frock heaved convulsively.

I reassured her eagerly. Those two great tears would have made me help to defraud all the ferry companies in the world.

A shilling would take her to Manly twice, I said, presenting her with two sixpences; and it would be a longer voyage. Suppose Frederick Thomas had another birthday to-morrow, and they went there?

She cried a little, in a quiet, subdued way, from relief, then she dried her eyes on the top of the cap, and gazed speech-lessly at the sixpences.

Anything so commonplace as "Thank you" she did not attempt to say, but she closed and unclosed her hand, where the little coins lay, and touched them with almost reverent fingers. Then she moved closer to me, and looked up with wet, shining eyes. "You can 'ave Frederick Thomas on your lap a bit," she said, in a low voice that had still a quiver in it.

H

I told her gently I would not like to disturb the little fellow,—he looked very comfortable where he was, and I should be getting out very soon.

We came up alongside the wharf at the quay, and I said good-bye to the children, took my penny out of my glove (a pernicious habit, but rife among ferry travellers of the gentler sex), and made my way across the gangway, up the jetty and through the turnstile, just as the Small Person staggered through with the large and lumpy Frederick clasped in her little arms.

When I was nearly at the top of the hill I found, to my horror, I had lost my purse. I distinctly remembered having it on my knee when I gave the sixpences, and therefore hurriedly retraced my steps. Frederick Thomas and the Small Person were still lingering, watching the water through the rails. " My purse ! " I gasped. " Did you see my purse ?—a brown one— my purse,—I have lost it."

The Small Person gave me a quick look

of comprehension. " Mebbe you dropped it—mebbe it's on the ship—'ere, 'old 'ard."

The next minute she had thrust the bulky Frederick into my astonished arms, had darted through the turnstile, heedless of the shout sent after her for her penny. I pressed closer to the opening and looked anxiously after her. The boat was moving off—there was quite a wide space of water between—but she sprang lightly over on to the deck, amid a perfect storm of cries and warnings.

Across the white-topped waves the steamer made its way, jauntily frothing up the water as if with supreme scorn at my *contretemps*.

For it was a *contretemps* without a doubt. Indeed, I cannot in all my life remember a time when I felt more abjectly unhappy, than I did as I stood on that quay, holding in my arms Frederick of the fat head and woollen cap.

People looked at me curiously as they came hurrying down for the boat ; several I knew by sight glanced at me and then at that awful child, with the greatest surprise depicted on their faces. For one thing, I knew I was not holding the boy just as a tender nurse should; he was terribly heavy, and I was simply grasping him round the waist just as I had taken him from the Small Person.

Ordinary babies seem to fall naturally into a sitting position on your arm, but this child had no joints, and just stayed in a stiff, shapeless heap. Once I tried to set him on the ground, but it was a failure. The Small Person had told me he was " gone in the legs," but this I had forgotten. The minute I tried to make him stand, however, his feet doubled under him, and he fell down helplessly. I gathered him up again, and with courage, born of utter despair, walked as far as the Neutral Bay shed. And then I saw some people I knew slightly crossing the quay, and I walked back to the North shore landing-place with burning cheeks.

If only I could have gone through and dropped him on one of the seats! I could have kept a watchful eye on him to see he didn't drown his hideous little self, and at the same time have appeared as if I had no connection with him. But I was absolutely penniless, and more than that, the man at the turnstile seemed to regard me with a distrustful eye. He had seen the Small Person in my company, and, of course, she had mulcted him of his penny.

I looked up at the clock. I had only had the child for four minutes, though it seemed an eternity since he had been thrust into my arms, and there was no chance of the boat coming back for another ten.

And I remembered there were only three shillings, two postage stamps, and a pearl button in my purse. I would rather have lost it ten times over than have endured this. My back was breaking with the unaccustomed burden. How the Small Person carried him about as she did will ever remain a mystery to me.

Dark thoughts entered my head of abandoning him, setting him down in a safe place on the ground, and stealthily fleeing citywards; but I knew officious people would raise a hue and cry after me, and I should be forced to take him again. I thought of tipping someone near to hold him, but then I had not the wherewithal to tip, and felt certain the little girl would not recover the purse.

Eight minutes still by the clock. The boy was slipping slowly from my arms. I gave him an impatient jerk upwards, and in so doing displaced his thumb from its mouth refuge. And then a fresh horror came upon me. His eyes disappeared in his fleshy cheeks, his head fell back, his face went purple, his mouth opened and exposed the red, naked gums, and a piercing and un-earthly yell arose from his throat. I stuffed his hand—nearly the whole of it—back into his mouth, and, almost choking with im-potent anger, bore him off beyond the Manly shed, where there seemed fewer people.

Someway the eight minutes dragged away —I have lived through whole weeks that have seemed far shorter—and the boat came back.

From my hiding place I watched the people stream off and disperse, thinking I would not go back till the coast was clearer. Suddenly I saw the Small Person flying over the ground to me like a little, wild rabbit.

Her eyes were dilated, her cheeks deathly pale, her lips twitching. She stretched out her little shaking arms.

"Guv 'im me, guv 'im me, at wanst," she said fiercely.

I dropped him upon her with the utmost promptitude, and she held him to her, almost hungrily.

"Well, did you get my purse," I said.

She gave me another fierce look from her blazing eyes, then she pulled it from the front of her dress and handed it to me.

"'Twas on the seat," she said shortly.

Then her anger burst out.

"An' I went back and saved it fer you an' all, an' then you go and try ter steal Frederick Thomas!"

" Try to—*what*? " I said, bewildered.

"Oh, I saw you; sneaking round here trying to hide from me."

She buried her nose in the pompon on the top of the cap, and down her cheeks there dropped two more great heavy tears like the tears of an old, sad woman. Frederick smiled up at her in his pleasing, toothless way, and tried playfully to insert his wet thumb in her eye.

She gathered him up tightly.

"Diddums den, tim tomothy," she said, smiling, too, a brief, watery smile. " Diddums try to steal my own Tom-tibithy ! "

" My *dear* child," I said, for this new aspect of the affair was appalling, "my *dear* child; why, I would sooner try to make off with the quay bodily than Frederick Thomas."

The Small Person gave me a look of withering and eloquent unbelief. Then she clasped Frederick Thomas close to her little breast, and moved silently and swiftly away with him

I watched the odd, small figure until it was lost in the grey, falling shadows of the winter afternoon.

And then I made my way, slowly and thoughtfully, up the hill, citywards, marvelling at the wonderful pennyworth it is possible to get on an everyday ferry-boat.

AS IT FELL OUT.

AS IT FELL OUT.

TWO loved her.

With the great love, that is. In her quiet home away out of one of the big country towns the lesser loves of mother, invalided sister, and delicate maiden aunts encompassed her, and made sweet all her days. She was a little idol to them all, now she was eighteen, having been delicate even to the point of death in her childhood.

It was the turning up of her schoolgirl curls and the lengthening of her frocks that brought the two with the boldness of business. Woolnough was a keeper of sheep, but Barrett was a tiller of the ground.

The mother and the maiden aunts favoured

Woolnough.   He was English, and his great
station was unmortgaged; but Bryda's eyes
were shyest when Barrett was there, and she
took more interest in the latest methods of
irrigation than the rise and fall of the wool
market.

In the heart of the keeper of sheep was
envy and hatred and bitterness, just as it
had been "in the beginning."

They smoked together one night after a
visit, and Woolnough's anger burst its
bounds.

"But for you, there would have been no
obstacle," he said.   "She was mine before
you came.   I have known her since she was
five.   I taught her to ride; she kissed me
for a little kangaroo I found for her when
she was ten; she even kissed me when she
was thirteen, and used to call herself my
little wife."

Redness, dull and deep, was on Barrett's
brow.

"She was a child," he said.   "She is
grown up now, and the choice lies with her."

As it Fell Out.

But Woolnough raved of the stealing of his darling, of the injustice, the deliberate planning of Barrett.

And Barrett's nature was the loyalest and sweetest in the world.

He knocked the ashes out of his pipe and stood up.

" I was going to ask her to-morrow," he said. " Since you think you have first right I will not go near for a week. After that, unless you have succeeded, I shall try again." Even as he spoke, however, his heart was warmed by the recollection of the sweet colour that had dyed her cheeks when she bade him good-bye.

On the seventh day after this, Bryda was dressed to go into Nerrinderie, for her weekly singing lesson. The busy little township lay ten miles away—one mile she always walked, which brought her to Booligabbili, where there was a platform siding; the rest of the way she went by train.

Now it happened that on this seventh day,

when she was dressed, even to her large white hat and pale grey dainty gloves, she fancied the plainness of her white muslin frock would receive an added charm from a bunch of pink roses in her waist-band.

" For," she whispered to her girlish heart, " Mr. Barrett will get in, perhaps, at the siding ; he nearly always goes in to the bank on Thursdays. And even if he doesn't—well, John Woolnough likes pretty things." She liked her old friend John very much, though she had told him twice that week she could not marry him.

The mother and the maiden aunts and the elder sister were still sitting over lunch in the shady dining-room. She went in to kiss them and say good-bye as usual, for this little weekly journey of hers was quite an event in their quiet stream of life.

They bade her keep in the shade of the fences, and be careful of the long grass. They begged her to walk slowly, and be very heedful getting in and out of the train. And to be *very* careful when she crossed any of the streets of Nerrinderie.

"Sweet little thing!" they said, almost before the door closed on her; "dear little thing! How beautiful she is! Wasn't she looking a little pale? Perhaps a tonic would do good. Sweet, little pretty thing!"

The pink roses ran in a riot of splendour over the lower fence of the cow paddock. Bryda went down and gathered the sweetest of them, tenderness in her eyes.

She remembered putting them in her waist belt, pinning a long stalk, and stooping for a pale, flushed exquisite bud that grew low down. She would put it in her brooch she thought, and if persuasively asked to give up the possession of it—well, the chances were she might come home without it.

It might have been five minutes later, it might have been an hour, that she was creeping through the quiet hall again with a face of death. Seeking her bedroom door and saying, "God! God! God!" with white lips and eyes wide with the terror of death.

1

Holding one little hand in the other, moaning softly, trembling, afraid to look.

But the death fear braced her in its awfulness, lent her quick, strange courage and calmness.

She tore away the muslin cuff of her sleeve. Two little marks were there, horribly distinct. She shut her eyes one moment to forget the slim, brown, loathsome thing that had touched her, and glided away under the rose growth.

Barrett had dreaded this for her; each fresh one he had seen this long, hot summer had filled him with fresh fear for her—every time he saw her, he begged her to be careful where she walked. Some weeks ago he had brought her a little case with a tiny hypodermic syringe in it, a bottle of strychnine, and full directions for its use. He had insisted upon giving her an object lesson on it; had made her work it, understand the measurements, and lose her fear of it.

It lay on her dressing table now, and she picked it up with steady fingers. Of course she must use it, and quickly, for what was that strange feeling creeping over her even now ? The directions swam before her eyes, but her brain served her. "Three to five minims if only a slight case," Barrett had said ; "ten if severe."

"I am not black in the face," she said, glancing at her white reflection in the glass.

So she drew up the rod to the mark of four, the needle in the strychnine, then she pinched up a piece of her poor little arm above the deadly bites, inserted the needle and pushed the piston down again. Then she slipped case and bottle into her pocket, and went to the door.

"I must certainly get to a doctor's," she muttered, and crept down the hall and out of the front door once more.

From the very first, she had known that she must not alarm those poor women in the dining room. One of her aunts had heart disease, the other was consumptive, the little mother was delicate, the sister had a sprained ankle. The servant had left the day before, and a successor not yet come.

"Dear, dear!" said an aunt at the window. "Why, the child must have come back for something; she is only just starting. Dear, dear, dear!—she is running, Mary, running in this shocking heat; it will half kill her."

At the gate of the little deserted platform Woolnough was standing. Even when he saw her white dress—she was not hurrying now—he did not go to meet her, for the bitterness of her last refusal was still in his heart, and he remembered Barrett was free to go to her.

But she fairly sprang at him.

"John," she said, "John! John! John! *John !*"

Her face was working, her eyes were full of wild horror. Now there was someone to help her, all her braveness fled away. She was like a little trembling child, terrified out of its life.

He flung his arm round her to steady

her, for she swayed towards him. The
shock of the strangeness of her manner
kept him dumb.

She leaned against him, clung to him.
"Help me," she said, "John! John! *John!*
help me!"

She thrust out her little wrist, and his face
went like death when he understood what
that ligature of gay sash ribbon meant.

He almost carried her into the waiting-
shed and put her on a seat.

"Did you see it?" he said.

"Brown," she answered, shudderingly.

He bound the ribbon tighter, he knelt
down and put his lips to the marks and
sucked with all his might.

She told him stutteringly what she had
done for herself.

"Strychnine!" he cried, "you injected
strychnine!—yourself!—where did you get
it?—great God! you may have killed
yourself!"

She motioned to her pocket. "Get it
out," she said.

He put his hand in, and found the case, the small bottle, the careful directions in Barrett's writing. And his heart leapt with the relief: he had the greatest faith in the cure himself, and he found she had not erred in the quantity.

" Four, you took? " he said. " I am going to give you another five—it must have been quite twenty minutes ago."

He injected it quickly, deftly, like one quite used to the method.

He almost cried aloud in his thankfulness when he saw the snake-poison symptoms abating under the powerful remedy. She was able to speak connectedly again; her pulse was better; the limpness was gone; the desire for sleep almost conquered. But he insisted upon walking her up and down the little shed; his arm was round her waist to give her support, she was clinging to his shoulder with both her hands.

And it fell out that Barrett saw them. His road had brought him into the enclosure on the opposite side of the little station.

He had come down, light-heartedly enough. Woolnough's surly manner when they met during the week made him certain his suit had been unsuccessful.

But he would not go from his word, and speak to her. When he saw the white fluttering dress come down the road, and noticed his rival leaning against the gates, he drew back among the bushes, and determined to jump unseen on the last car, when the train came. He even walked back along the tree-hidden road for a little way, and smoked a pipe of great peace.

When the train was due, he strolled back again, and saw Woolnough on his knees by her side. Again he swung round and walked away. A flush was on his forehead: he felt he owed Woolnough an apology for looking. But his contentment and quiet spirit had gone. What if she yielded to this last appeal of the man?—What if it had been mere friendliness in her manner that he had mistaken for a token that she cared a little?

He waited away for a little time, his back turned.

The train was already ten minutes overdue. When he heard the far-off rumble, he turned his face to the station again—the man must be off his knees by now. And his eyes looked straight before him into the waiting-shed.

Stupor came creeping slowly over the girl again.

"John," she said faintly.

He drew her closer. "What is it, little girl?"

She hid her face a minute in his sleeve.

"Is there no one on the station?" she whispered. "Mr. Barrett—or—anyone; please look."

The poor child felt she might die at the doctor's, and longed inexpressibly for Barrett to be with her.

John looked.

And saw the man's deathly-white face through the bushes opposite, saw the wild eyes, and knew how they were interpreting this thing.

But he had snatched her back from death for himself. His arm tightened around her waist.

"No," he said in an even tone. "There is no one on the station, Bryda."

Then the train rushed up, and they went away in it to the doctor's.

And Barrett turned slowly round and walked up the hill again to his home.

   *   *   *   *

To this day the mother, the maiden aunts, and the sister think Bryda stayed that night unexpectedly in Nerrinderie, merely to keep her old schoolfellow, the doctor's daughter, company.

How were they to guess of the wild night's struggle for their darling's life, which had been fought between skill and death? Or of the wonderful day in which, when the dawn crept in, the rod Death held had burst out into blossoms of amaranth?

They thought her pale, perhaps, when Woolnough drove her home — the heat yesterday, of course, and the running. How could she have been so unwise as to run? And did she know she had left the slip-rails down in the cow paddock, and there had been no milk for tea?

Bryda cried under the bed-clothes every night for a week, when she heard Barrett had gone away. Gone off to Coolgardie, report said, and sold the farm—which never was much good—to a neighbouring squatter.

Then she grew ashamed of herself, and pride stepped in, and made her gay again. And, in the end, it fell out that she married Woolnough.

ALMOST AN IDYLL.

ALMOST AN IDYLL.

BUT for four things, the "almost" might have been left out of the title. They were very trivial things, too—mere details; but still they took from the symmetry and exquisite completeness we are wont to look for in an idyll.

The heroine had freckles—quite a thick powdering of them on her smooth cheeks and the bridge of her nose. That was the first thing.

For the second, the hero wore a black coat, rather shiny at the seams, and frayed at the wrists—the kind of coat that one associates with a high stool and ledger, luncheon sandwiches (newspaper wrapped), and a boarding house at a pound a-week.

In perfect idylls nothing but white flannel jackets are allowed.

The third detracting factor was the absence of forks. Somebody had forgotten them in the confusion consequent upon packing up for a week's picnic. And neither fingers nor chopsticks, when used in conjunction with corned beef, fish, or potatoes, are precisely idyllic.

The fourth thing was Ebenezer. Nothing else, however, in the world was wanting.

There was water, wind-kissed, dancing, bubbling with laughter and light; water, brown and red and shadowy with suns that died gloriously; water, pure and silver white, smiling up to a full-faced moon.

And there were skies, beautiful always; great, high, wide fields of delicate tints, with never a chimney nor brick monstrosity across their loveliness.

Trees? Miles of them! Green young gums, greener young gums, young gums almost white in their delicate pale greenness. Old gums, sturdy and fearless, sun-smitten

brown and deepest red; older gums, silvered
as to trunk, and with grey, bleached leaves
on edge, chary of casting shade. Ti-trees,
sober - green and ragged; wattle, fresher
green and yellow crowned; trees grown
blue and more blue, merging into the grey-
blue tenderness of distant hills.

And there was growing life in plenty.

Even the chaperone, who was forty, was
young. You had only to look in her eyes
to discover that.

But the heroine was deliciously young.

If you had been artistically inclined, you
would have seized a canvas and tried to
catch her upon it with a flash and quick
flutter of brushes. And you would have
called your picture "Spring," or "Young
Hope," or "Glad Life," or "The Spirit of
a New World," or some such commonplace
title, because the paucity of language would
not allow you to express better her sur-
prising youth and vigour.

Her blood was young, and her slight,
straight body. Her lips were young—their

redness and freshness were marvellous.
Every curl and loose tress of her hair had
a glad, mysterious secret with the wind,
because it was also very young; and her
eyes were brimming with that light and
happiness seen in very young eyes only.

She had freckles, certainly, as I said
before, but then they were very young, too,
having been born during the picnic, and it
was only because the sun knew she was a
child of earth at its happiest that he had
kissed her, again and again, in his gladness.

Fresh blouses, muslins and shady hats,
flannels, blazers and head-gear uncity-like,
white tents, gaily painted boats, and abound-
ing happiness, made up the background and
the foreground and the middle distance of the
most sunshiny picture the great artist—the
world—had sketched for himself for Christmas amusement. But the second and the
fourth detail, the black coat and Ebenezer,
were shadows he had skilfully placed in, because, like the wielders of smaller brushes,
he also knew a thing or two about contrasts

and relief and the like. And the highest light being Rhoda—Ebenezer and the coat did excellently well for dull, deep shadows.

The coat was Ebenezer's. That, of course.

As if anyone else there would have shiny seams and threadbare buttons; as if anyone else would have black at all!

Ebenezer was the man with the black coat. *That*, of course.

As if anyone else in that gay, modern-spirited crowd would have been burdened with such a name!

He did not like it himself, and often thought his parents might have chosen more happily. But somehow he never seemed to have the time or inclination to change it. All his life had been so taken up in fighting the world, which for its own artistic purposes insisted that he should be a shadow.

He was very ordinary to look at. His hair was brown, quite dull, and without a suspicion of wave. His skin was dull: high stools, alternated with boarding-houses,

K

seldom improve the complexion; his chin,
his nose, and his forehead were altogether
unremarkable. His eyes were dull—at any
rate they were quiet, and the shadow showed
there most of all.

It seemed odd that he should be there at
all among those laughter-loving picnickers.
But one of them had rubbed up against him
in life, and felt a happy man's pity for his
loneliness and dulness. He asked him what
he was going to do with the holiday week.

Ebenezer didn't know—smoke, he sup-
posed, on the lounge, as none of the other
lodgers would be using it.

The Happy Man was engaged to the best
and loveliest woman on earth, and the two of
them were going, with other happy ones,
Hawkesbury Riverwards to camp, and be
nomads for the festive days. And they were
sorry for all the world because it was not
themselves. So they asked Ebenezer to
come, because they were afraid the Fates
would stick pins into them, if they did not
spread their happiness a little.

Ebenezer said " No," of course.

Then the leg of the lounge came off, and his tobacco was dry and didn't taste. And the long terraces opposite were peeling in the sun, and no constable-like wind bade the still, hot air in the streets " move on."

So the last day, when the Happy Man asked him to change his mind, he did so, to his own absolute amazement. He packed a little bag with a few clothes, bought a pair of sand shoes, to save his office boots, and held his head quite jauntily when he informed his landlady he was going for "a week's holi-day." But by the end of the first day, he was overpoweringly sorry he had come. He would have given a whole month's salary— six golden pounds—to have been able to get away from them all, back to the narrow lodging-house in the hot, noisy street. But a launch had brought them there, and a launch would call for them at the end of the time. There was no getting away before.

So he gave himself up to the inevitable. He sculled the chaperone about the river

She was the only one of the party with whom he did not feel intensely awkward and miserable. And he took the billy-boiling as his own particular work. The stick-hunting, the manipulation of the tripod, the water fetching, and the watching for the first steam — all these were occupations that disposed of his time and his awkward hands. He could never have endured that week had it not been for the extraordinary tea-drinking capacity of the party.

At night they all went out in the boats and floated dreamily about in the white moonlight, and lifted their happy voices, and sang of love and roses and clasped hands and kisses.

And the wind whispered the same things, and the trees caught the low, sweet secret, and whispered it in turn to the sky, that looked on with all its tender, shining eyes.

And the beautiful river listened and laughed joyfully as it lay in the arms of its lover, the shore.

And Ebenezer sat with his pipe gone out, and listened, too.

The first night he had ventured out with them, and had sat silent at the end of the boat while they sang to the music of the plashing oars. And he had been drunk with the beauty of it all. The girls, with their soft, white dresses and moonlit eyes, the little, leaping silver waves, the swaying, whispering trees, the rising and falling of the sweet voices—no wonder they were like intoxicants to his unaccustomed senses.

Rhoda had been nearest to him, once the wind had blown a fold of her muslin dress across his knee, three times she had spoken to him in her young friendliness. So, in return, he gave her all his heart.

Secretly, of course. He had the wisdom to know that hearts are utterly useless appendages when backed by only seventy-two pounds a year.

That is why he stayed on shore after the first night, and let the wind blow little bursts of song and soft laughter across the water into his face. He said he was afraid the billy might be stolen if he went again: he would stay and be watchdog, since he could not help in the singing.

His pipe nearly always went out as soon as they were fairly started, and he used to sit staring out after them into the white darkness, till, some hours later, they pulled slowly back.

Sometimes he used to feel supremely sorry for himself because of the new burden that had fallen upon him, but that was generally when the boats had drifted out of sight and hearing.

Other times he hugged himself in the glad, exultant feeling that he had given his heart to the beautiful girl out there in the boat, and that she knew nothing about it.

He assured himself that reciprocated love could never be love in the very highest sense.

But he nearly always laughed as he said it.

During the long, hushed evenings by the water edge, he found out what his ideas of heaven were.

It was a river, he decided, a river that flowed to Eternity. And it had a sky above it filled with white stars and one white great moon.

And his own particular heaven would be a small boat with Rhoda in it, Rhoda in a white dress with flannel flowers in her hair. Rhoda just opposite to him, with the steering lines in her hands to keep them from running into any of the angels who would have been infinitely in the way.

On the fifth evening the Mighty Artist scooped up some white in his great brush. He fancied a dash of it, clear and untoned across the shadow might be more effective even than his first design.

Ebenezer asked the chaperone if she would let him pull her up the river. It was just at the finish of tea, and they were all sitting in lazy scatteredness about the grass.

She told him she was good for three more cups of tea yet, but not for the exertion of getting into a boat.

" I'll come," Rhoda said, with sudden impulsiveness.   "I'm tired of seeing people eat—shall I?"

"Yes," he said.

He went down to the sand stretch a little way off and got the boat ready with trembling hands. He moved the seat half-a-dozen times; he baled out every drop of water, and laid down the scrap of carpet.

That he should have his heaven so soon as this!

She came down to the edge, and he helped her in, placed the steering-lines in her hands, and pushed off with her from the very spot where he had sat each night.

Long after he remembered that he hardly spoke at all. She sat there looking at him with her kind, young eyes, talking, laughing, bidding him look now at the purple-gold edge of the sun, almost gone; now at the moon stealing up behind the trees; now at the fish that leapt from the water for a second; now at flock of black swan overhead.

He listened to her, and looked at her, and forgot the river did not flow to Eternity.

By-and-bye his strange silence quieted her. She thought, perhaps, he did not care to talk, so she slipped her hand over the side into the cool, moving water, and gave herself up to the thought of beautiful love that some day would come into her life, and of shining days that would stretch out over all her future.

The moon rose higher and the river grew white and more white; and still he rowed on and on, and still she leaned back and thought of love with parted lips and tender eyes.

Then a fish jumped close to her hand, and she remembered Ebenezer was in the boat.

"It is late—let us go back, Ebenezer," she said, dreamily.

She did not notice she used his Christian name—they all called him by it when speaking of him, since it was so odd, but he noticed, and was reconciled to it for ever after.

He rowed back again over the silver stretches and the shadowed ones. He thought the moon had never been so large nor the stars so shiningly countless.

Then they came up to the strip of pale sand, and he made the boat fast and lifted her out without a word.

All the sixth day was warm and bright from the recollection of it.

The seventh day they were to break up the camp and go home.   Ebenezer began to prepare a little chamber in his heart for the reception of the romance of his life.

It was swept clean from every other thought ; it was lonely, infinitely sad ; it was a little inward grave, and he had a key ready to lock it, and make it a thing apart all his life from the other chambers that were not hallowed.

Then the artist grew capricious.   Give a little child a book of black and white illus- trations and a paint box, and notice the way it will load the brightest paints upon the figures that are the blackest.

The artist forgot Art, and became even as a little child.

Almost an Idyll.

He filled his brush with all the colours that are in the sunset, in the brightening dawn, in happy human hearts, in hope at its birth.

A man came up in his sailing boat and joined the party. He was fulfilling a promise to join them on the last day, and he had brought all the letters that had accumulated for everybody in town.

He dealt them out, slowly, teasingly—bills, invitations, love letters, circulars.

There was one for Ebenezer—fat, closely-written.

He took it and went down to the sand-strip to read it in solitude and surprise; he who had never before got a letter of this length!

The Happy Man saw his look of astonishment, and hoped nothing was wrong.

"It's from a fellow in the office," Ebenezer said, staring at the signature. He turned away and went down to his old seat at the water edge.

Rhoda found him there two hours later

when tea was half over. The others sent
her down to see if all was right, as she was
the youngest.

He told her all about it ; asked her to read
the letter and tell him for certain that he was
not dreaming.

"Robinson might be playing a practical
joke on me, you see," he said, "and perhaps
my brain is not clear enough to detect it."

But Rhoda's was not, either, for everything was simple and bore truth on the face
of it.

Robinson had entered into a sweep that
had to do with the Melbourne Cup. He had
taken two £1 tickets, but, before the event
was run, an evil time came upon him, and
he needed twenty shillings in cash more than
he had ever needed money on earth.   So
Ebenezer, in one of the weak moments he
was subject to, despite his shabby coat,
offered to lend him that sum.   Robinson
told him he might never be able to pay him
back, and asked him if, instead, he would
buy one of his two consultation tickets.

Ebenezer had never gone into a sweep in his life. It startled him a little—not that he objected on principle to that mode of gambling, but that he had hitherto felt it was one of the luxuries which might be indulged in only by people with incomes greater than £72.

Still, Robinson was a good fellow and in sore trouble. He would not accept the loan, so of course there was nothing for it but to buy the ticket.

" Which will you have ? " Robinson said, " 690, or 10,009 ? "

Ebenezer laughed and said, " Either or either," pronouncing the first word with an initial " e " and the second with an " i."

" Keep it for me," he added, " and when the results are out you, can just pay any fortune I may have made into my bank, where I have a balance of £4 at present."

So Robinson put the tickets away in his desk in separate envelopes, labelling one with his own name, the other with his friend's.

And Ebenezer forgot forthwith the whole

matter, and could no more have told the number of either of the tickets than the number of stars in the heavens.

In course of time the race came off.

" No luck," Robinson said, and Ebenezer did not even sigh, for he had never dreamed of expecting it.

After that, Robinson left the office and disappeared altogether.

This strange, long letter Ebenezer was reading by the edge of the little, lapping, river waves, was from him.

"One of those two tickets drew a big prize," it said, "a prize of £10,000. It happened to be yours, Ebenezer, number 690, which I had marked with your name; 10,009, my number, was a blank. I believe I was meant originally for an honest man. Up till then I had always been able to show clean hands through life. But my strength was not as my days, though the great, good Book tells us it shall be.

"There was a woman I had wanted with all the life and soul of me for years. With money she was possible. And with something less than a crime—for you had told me to choose the tickets—wealth undreamed of would be mine, and she would come to me. So of course I took it, Ebenezer. There is nothing the best man on God's earth would not do with a love like mine in his heart. Not that you will understand or know anything about it, men like you never do, Eben, my friend.

"However, she played me false four days ago, and she's gone to America with a bridegroom worth treble that wretched sweep. So, of course, the money's no good to me any longer—nor life, either.

"I have placed the former, less ten per cent., to your banking account of £1. The latter I shall return without delay to the God who gave it. Buy a new coat, old man, first thing with the money—that black one of yours is deucedly shabby. Then get a wife. A young one who doesn't know enough to deceive you. And, for the love of heaven, smoke a better tobacco. God bless you!"

Just as Rhoda finished this wonderful letter the Happy Man came along. He had the *Evening News* in his hand.

" R'mber Robinson ? " he said to Ebenezer. " Cove with fine moustache,—awfully gone on Rosina Delarne in the Opera Company. He's blown his brains out, poor beggar ! "

They did'nt break up the camp on the right day after all.

Ebenezer's nature was slow, and this sudden upheaval of his life almost stopped it. For a few days he was ill enough to make moving him unwise. There was a doctor in the party, and he stayed on, also the chaperone, the Happy Man and his fiancée, and Rhoda, who was the fiancée's sister—the rest went home. Rhoda helped to nurse him, read to him out in the sunshine, coaxed him into eating what was ordered, encouraged him to talk of that part of his life that had been bottled up, and listened to it with tears of quick young pity in her eyes.

So the idyll closed in a consistently idyllic fashion.